NEW HAVEN PUBLIC LIBRARY

W9-AJP-956

Candy Shop

Jan Wahl

Illustrated by Nicole Wong

ıİı **Charlesbridge**

E WAHL
Candy shop /
35000094002671 CHILDREN'S ROOM
MAIN

To Stan and Marilyn Adamski—J. W.
For Dan—N. W.

Text copyright © 2004 by Jan Wahl
Illustrations copyright © 2004 by Nicole Wong
All rights reserved, including the right of reproduction in whole or in part in any form.
Charlesbridge and colophon are registered trademarks of Charlesbridge Publishing, Inc.

Published by Charlesbridge
85 Main Street
Watertown, MA 02472
(617) 926-0329
www.charlesbridge.com

Library of Congress Cataloging-in-Publication Data

Wahl, Jan.
  Candy shop / Jan Wahl ; illustrated by Nicole Wong.
     p. cm.
Summary: When a boy and his aunt find that a bigot has written something on the side-
walk outside the candy shop owned by a new immigrant from Taiwan, they set out to
comfort the owner.
ISBN 1-57091-508-3 (reinforced for library use)
[1. Toleration—Fiction. 2. Taiwanese Americans—Fiction. 3. Stores, Retail—Fiction.]
I. Wong, Nicole E., ill. II. Title.
PZ7.W1266Can 2004
[E]—dc21   2003003695

Printed in Korea
(hc) 10 9 8 7 6 5 4 3 2 1

Illustrations done in mixed media on Fabriano cold press paper
Display type set in Chestnut and text type set in Monotype Baskerville
Color separated, printed, and bound by Sung In Printing, South Korea
Production supervision by Linda Jackson
Designed by Susan Mallory Sherman

I'm a cowboy,

riding my horse through our backyard,
chasing buffalo. Aunt Thelma
stands at the door.
"Is that any way to get sweeping done?"
she yells. "If you want to earn any money,
you'd better get busy." She chuckles.

When I'm done, Aunt Thelma gives me two quarters.
She's going shopping. I'm going, too.
I've got a sweet tooth to satisfy at
the Candy Shop.
I've saved a dollar fifty to spend.

She brushes my hair,
makes me put on a shirt and wash my hands
and wear shoes.

It's hot. Shops are two blocks away.
On the next street, they don't grow
many trees. Men sit on porches.
Some houses are boarded up.
We walk faster.
There are empty lots.
On our street we keep the yards looking fine.
Aunt Thelma hums one of those old hymns.
I know it, too. One more block!

First, Aunt Thelma takes me to the Bon Ton,
where she buys a hat and umbrella.
I pull at her skirt. "When do we visit
the Candy Shop?" I ask.
"Take it easy. Candy won't go away," she says.

I chase the store calico cat around.
I pretend it's a fierce mountain lion.

Back outside, Aunt Thelma waves at people.
"See you in church!" she calls.
I stare at round red juicy apples in
front of Tichenor's grocery.
One apple costs 25¢.

I buy one for me and one for Aunt Thelma.
That leaves a dollar to spend.
I pull Aunt Thelma with her umbrella
down the sunny street.
"Not so fast!" she giggles.

I can't wait. I shout, "I want
candy. LET'S GO!"
I let out a cowboy yell to scare two dogs. "Yee-Ha!"
The dogs are coyotes.
I need a haircut, she tells me. . . .

At Fuzzy Williams' barbershop I sit
high up wrapped in a sheet.
Everything there smells of witch hazel.
Makes me dizzy.
"A cowboy doesn't get his hair cut," I growl.
Aunt Thelma laughs. "He does
if I am his aunt."

My sweet tooth is hungry.
We pass by the U-Need-A Used Book Store.
Next to it is the Second Hand Shop with
a yellow baby buggy in the window,
missing a wheel.

On the other side of the street is my
favorite place—the Candy Shop.

The owner, Miz Chu, peers out the door.
She's from Taiwan. What's this?
On the sidewalk a lot of people are gathering.
Do they all want candy, I wonder?
No—they stare at something written
on the sidewalk.

I can't see it but it makes Miz Chu cry.
Aunt Thelma pushes through the crowd
with her new umbrella.
We step inside.

Miz Chu looks scared.
"Honey," Aunt Thelma whispers, "don't
pay no never mind. There's mean,
nasty folk in the world, but
most are fine as gold."
She puts an arm around Miz Chu.
My aunt is large. Miz Chu is small.

I look at those wonderful candies, for I don't
know what else to do.
In glass cases in neat rows are open boxes
of peppermints, licorice whips—red
and black, jawbreakers, cherry drops,
lemon drops, malted milk balls,
suckers, peanut brittle, rock
candy on strings, peanut clusters,
taffy, candy corn, gumdrops,
jelly beans, and a whole bunch more.

I tip my hat to Miz Chu.
That's what a cowboy does!
Aunt Thelma tries to calm her.
Miz Chu dries her eyes with a nice polka-dot
hanky from Aunt Thelma. She always
keeps an extra.

A cowboy would chase those people away.
He couldn't just stand here. He'd
do something.

Quick as the wind I rush to the closet next to
the sink to fetch pail, soap, brush.
I run water into the pail, go out
to the sidewalk, and on my knees scrub
away dumb words as hard as I can.

Now Aunt Thelma comes out to shake
her new umbrella at the people.
"Shoo, GET ALONG! Don't you got places
where they want you?"

Nobody knows who wrote the words.
At last the crowd leaves and Aunt Thelma hugs me.
I cry, too. What's happening?

I follow my aunt into the shop.
Miz Chu comes up to me.
"Here, Daniel," she says. "Hold this."
Slowly she picks out candy and puts it
in the tall, red-striped sack.

I follow my aunt into the shop.
Miz Chu comes up to me.
"Here, Daniel," she says. "Hold this."
Slowly she picks out candy and puts it
in the tall, red-striped sack.

She doesn't want my four shiny quarters.

Aunt Thelma smiles. "Tell you what,"
she says quietly.
She wants to say something.
"Come share sweet potato pie."
She makes the best sweet potato pie
in the whole world.
Miz Chu locks up. Then she takes my hand,
and proudly we take her home.

MAR 2006